I Don't Want a Cold!

Licensed by The Illuminated Film Company
Based on the LITTLE PRINCESS animation series © The Illuminated Film Company 2007
Made under licence by Andersen Press Ltd., London
'I Don't Want a Cold!' episode written by Cas Willing
Producer Iain Harvey.   Director Edward Foster
© The Illuminated Film Company/Tony Ross 2007
Design and layout © Andersen Press Ltd., 2007.
Colour separated, printed and bound in China by Midas Printing Ltd.
10   9   8   7   6   5   4   3   2
British Library Cataloguing in Publication Data available.

ISBN: 978 1 84270 655 8

This book has been printed on acid-free paper

I Don't Want a Cold!

Tony Ross

Andersen Press · London

The sun was shining as the cockerel crowed in the morning, but everyone in the castle was asleep. Everyone apart from the Little Princess.

"I'll need my hat," she giggled, "and my sunglasses."

It was the day of the royal picnic and the Little Princess was very excited. She started to blow up her rubber ring, when…

"A-tishoo!"

The Little Princess sneezed so hard the ring was sent flying across the room.

"Wake up! It's picnic day!" cried the Little Princess as she rushed into her parents' bedroom. The King and Queen stopped snoring and rubbed their eyes.

"A-tishoo!" sneezed the Little Princess.

There were more snuffles over breakfast.

"Can we go now?" asked the Little Princess.

"Slow down, sweetheart," yawned the Queen. "I haven't finished… eurgh!"

The King pointed to his daughter's runny nose.

"Give it a blow, poppet."

The Chef and the Maid were enjoying a
lovely cup of tea in the castle kitchen.

"PICNIC TIME!"

bellowed the Little Princess.
The Maid spluttered into her
drink then got up to start packing.

"This is my best day!" grinned the Little Princess when she skipped outside. The whole royal household trailed behind her, loaded down with hampers, rugs and picnic food.

The Little Princess had chosen a picnic spot right next to the royal pond. "Can I go in now?"
When the Maid nodded, she shrieked with joy and raced towards the water.

"Couugghhh!"

The King and Queen put down their iced buns and looked at each other. First sneezes, then a runny nose, now a cough…

The Maid plucked the Little Princess out of the water.
The picnic was promptly re-packed and they marched
back to the castle.
The Little Princess was furious.
"But I want to paddle!"

"No paddling for sick princesses."

"I'm not sick," argued the Little Princess,

"A-tishooOO!"

The Maid frowned. "Cover your mouth when you sneeze or you'll spread all those nasty germs."

The Doctor listened to the Little Princess's chest.
"The Princess has caught a cold," she announced.
"Why is it called a cold when I feel so hot?"
asked the Little Princess.
"She must go to bed," continued the Doctor,
"and she must stay there."

The Little Princess was tucked up before she'd even had lunch.
"No getting up now," reminded the King.
The Little Princess's picnic day
was going terribly wrong.

The next morning the Little Princess was still full of cold.
She'd been coughing, sneezing and spluttering for hours.
By the afternoon the Little Princess had nothing left to sneeze.
"I've got room for some food now," she decided. "I'm HUNGRY!"

"The Princess is hungry!" cried the Maid, running to the kitchen.

The Chef kissed his fingertips in delight.

"I have the perfect thing!"

The Little Princess was horrified.
"What's that?"
"Broth," said the Maid.
"I don't want broth, I want a picnic,"
scowled the Little Princess.
But she was so hungry she ate it
anyway. The Little Princess felt
very sorry for herself.

Everyone else was outside having fun in the garden, while she was stuck in bed.

"It's no fun being sick," she moaned.

"I know!" cried the Little Princess. "I'll have a picnic in bed!"
She straightened the covers and reached under the mattress
for her toys. Soon they were all dressed and lined up around a
spotty hanky picnic rug.
"This is Mummy…" she announced…"and this is Daddy."

The Little Princess giggled then wedged
her sunhat over Scruff's ears.
"I'm me and that's the Admiral."
All she needed now was her tea set,
but it was too far away to reach.

The Little Princess leant over the bed and rummaged around for her umbrella. It was just the thing she needed to hook her dolly's pram! She quickly climbed aboard, then rolled across the bedroom.

"Princess!"

called a firm voice behind her. The Little Princess turned to see the Doctor standing in the doorway, accompanied by the rest of the royal household.

"But my feet never touched the floor," said the Little Princess.

"I don't have a cold any more," announced the Little Princess.

"Puss has it."

"Cats can't get people colds," said the Doctor.

The Little Princess put her hands on her hips.

"Well I haven't got it."

The Doctor listened into her stethoscope for ages.

Everyone held their breath. "You're right," she announced finally.

"The cold has gone."

The Little Princess clapped her hands.

"Yes! We can go on our picnic!"

she shrieked.

Everyone trooped back outside with the picnic things.
The excited Little Princess pulled on her armbands and
headed straight for the pond.

"Atishoo!" sneezed the Maid.
The Little Princess stopped in her tracks.

"Atishoo!" sneezed the King and the Queen.

"Atishoo!" sneezed the General. And the Chef. And the
Prime Minister. Even the Admiral couldn't help joining in.

The Little Princess gasped. "You're all sick!"
Nobody said a single word. "Bed for all of you!"
she cried, shooing them away from the picnic.
The King frowned. "It's not fair."

The Little Princess led the way back to the castle, while the grown-ups coughed and spluttered behind her.

"Come on, Mum. Come on, Dad, no picnics for you!"

The picnic was over before it had begun, but the Little
Princess wasn't disappointed. Now she was the one in charge.
"This is much more fun," she grinned, handing the General
a hot water bottle.

The Chef wrapped his blanket round his shoulders and started
to creep quietly out of the parlour.
"Hey!" cried the Little Princess. "No getting up…

...your broth's waiting for you!"